The Princess and the Pea

A Puffin Easy-to-Read Classic

retold by Harriet Ziefert

illustrated by Emily Bolam

PUFFIN BOOKS

PUFFIN BOOKS

Published by the Penguin Group

Penguin Books USA Inc., 375 Hudson Street, New York, New York 10014, U.S.A.

Penguin Books Ltd, 27 Wrights Lane, London W8 5TZ, England

Penguin Books Australia Ltd, Ringwood, Victoria, Australia

Penguin Books Canada Ltd, 10 Alcorn Avenue, Toronto, Ontario, Canada M4V 3B2

Penguin Books (N.Z.) Ltd, 182–190 Wairau Road, Auckland 10, New Zealand

Penguin Books Ltd, Registered Offices: Harmondsworth, Middlesex, England

First published in the United States of America by Viking,
a division of Penguin Books USA Inc., 1996

Published simultaneously in Puffin Books

7 9 10 8

THE LIBRARY OF CONGRESS HAS CATALOGED THE VIKING EDITION AS FOLLOWS:

Ziefert, Harriet.
The princess and the pea / retold by Harriet Ziefert; illustrated by Emily Bolam.
p. cm.—(Viking easy-to-read)
"A Viking easy-to-read classic."
Adaptation of: Prindsessen paa aerten / H.C. Andersen.
Summary: The queen has a plan to help the prince find a real princess to marry.
ISBN 0-670-86054-9
[1. Fairy tales.] I. Bolam, Emily, ill. II. Andersen, H.C. (Hans Christian), 1805-1875.
Prindsessen paa aerten. English. III. Title.
IV. Series.
PZ8.Z54Pr 1996 [E]—dc20 95-39341 CIP AC

Puffin Books ISBN 0-14-038083-3

Printed in the United States of America

Puffin® and Easy-to-Read® are registered trademarks of Penguin Books USA Inc.

Reading Level 1.8

The Princess and the Pea

There once was a prince,
who wanted to marry a princess.
But she had to be a *real* princess.

The prince looked and looked.
He met many princesses.

Many, many princesses!
Many, many, many princesses!

But the prince sent
all of them away.
He did not think they
were *real* princesses.

One day there was a big storm.
A princess knocked at the door.

"Come in," said the king.
"Come in," said the queen.

Oh, what a drippy princess!

Her hair was drippy!

Her dress was drippy!

Her shoes were
drippy!

But still she said
she was a *real* princess.

The queen said, "I will see.
I will see if this is a *real* princess."
And she went off to make the bed.

First the queen
put a tiny pea
under the mattress.

Next, the queen put
1...2...3...4...5...
6...7...8...9...10...
mattresses on top of the pea.

Then she put
1...2...3...4...5...
6...7...8...9...10 more
mattresses on top of them.

On top of the twenty mattresses,
the queen put twenty down covers.

Then she called the princess.
"Your bed is ready!" she said.

The princess went to bed.

Oh, what a sleepy princess!

In the morning the queen asked,
"How did you sleep?"

And the king asked,
"How did you sleep?"

And the prince asked,
"How did you sleep?"

"I did not sleep,"
said the princess.
"I did not sleep at all!
I did not sleep because there
was a big lump in my bed."

The queen smiled.
The king smiled.

"You must be a *real*
princess!" they said.

"Only a *real* princess could feel a pea under twenty mattresses!"

The prince married the princess, because he knew she was a *real* princess!

And the pea?
They saved it for ever and ever.